To Lucy

Published by World's Work Ltd
The Windmill Press, Kingswood, Tadworth, Surrey
Layout and design by The Romany Studio Workshop
Reproduced by Graphic Affairs Ltd, Southend
Printed in Great Britain by
William Clowes (Beccles) Limited, Beccles and London
SBN 437 66172 5

Hopfellow

JENNY PARTRIDGE

A WORLD'S WORK CHILDREN'S BOOK

Hopfellow the frog was dozing contentedly
in the sunshine on the riverbank
when he was awakened by a sudden jerk
on the end of his fishing line.

"My!" he cried, "this must be a big one!"
He pulled hard, and out came
an old boot covered in weeds.
"Well, I can't cook that for my dinner."
The sound of giggling made him spin
round.

"Hallo, young scallywags!" he called, as Verity Twitcher and the Pollensnuff twins, Amy and Pippin, appeared behind him. "What are you three up to today?"
"Nothing," they sighed. "We're bored."

"Bored?" exclaimed Hopfellow.
"Why, when I was your age,
I played on the river all day long!"
"But what did you *do*, Mr Hopfellow?"
asked Pippin.

"Ah," replied the frog dreamily,
"my cousin Quilp and I used to have
the most marvellous boat races."
"But we don't have a boat,"
said Verity sadly.
"Come with me," cried Hopfellow,
"and I'll show you how to make your own."

Under the tall horse-chestnut trees,
several large prickly green shells
lay on the grass.

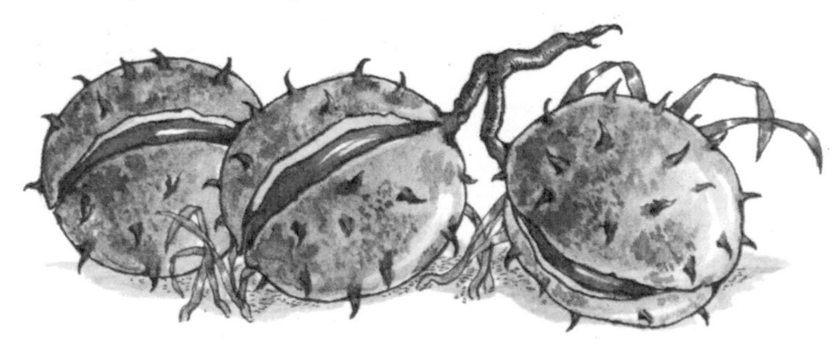

"There," said Hopfellow,
pointing to one.
"Now, who could wish
for a finer boat?"

Hopfellow showed them how to carry
the shells on their heads, back to the river.
"I can't see where I'm going!"
squeaked Amy.

The frog carefully fitted a long twig inside each shell boat to make a mast. "Now for the sails," he said. "Fetch me my newspaper, Verity."

"There you are, jolly sailors," he cried, launching the little boats. "In you jump!" They scrambled into their shells, chattering happily to each other. "Right," shouted Hopfellow from the bank. "First one to reach the bridge is the winner. GO!"

Using their paws as paddles, they splashed along, laughing and squealing.

"Out of my way, Pippin!" cried Amy, "or I'll bump into you." Their little boats collided, and almost capsized. "Ugh," spluttered Pippin, "my tail is all wet – look out, here comes Verity!"

Hopfellow ran along the riverbank, calling, "Careful now Verity, don't lean over too far or you'll fall in."
Verity was a caterpillar's length in front of the twins, and paddling very fast.

“I’m winning,” she shouted, “I’m the best sailor!” She bounced about excitedly, rocking the boat from side to side until suddenly it overturned, throwing her into the water. “Help,” she gasped. “Oh, help!”

Hopfellow grabbed his fishing line
and raced to the little bridge.
"Don't panic, Verity!
I'll soon have you out of there."

He cast his line; the fish hook caught
in the belt of her dress and he lifted her,
dripping, out of the water.

The others stared at poor Verity
as she dangled in mid-air.
Hopfellow hauled her up on to the bridge,
and put his coat around her.

"I don't know what your Grandmother
will say. You'd better come back with me
and dry yourself."

The twins paddled to the bank, and climbed out of their boats. "Oh Verity you did look funny!" giggled Pippin.

"Now, now," said Hopfellow,
"I think Verity has learnt her lesson.
Come on, back to my cottage
for the finest tea you have ever had."

They all hurried to Hopfellow's house, snuggled under the water forget-me-nots.

Hopfellow made the tea and the children
put their wet clothes by the fire to dry.
"Ouch," cried Verity as Amy rubbed her

with Hopfellow's roughest bath towel.
"I'm sure a large slice of blackberry pie
will make you feel better," said the frog.

It was indeed a wonderful tea.
Afterwards Hopfellow lit his pipe
and told them tales of his adventures
on the riverbank.

It sounded so exciting that Verity
and the twins felt a little ashamed
that they had ever said they were bored.

"I think it's time you went home now,"
said Hopfellow when their clothes
were dry again.

"Oh," cried the twins, "can we come again, and sail our boats, Mr Hopfellow?" "Of course," smiled the frog, "but next time

I must teach you to be better sailors –
what do you say Verity?"
"Atishoo!" she sneezed, and everyone
burst out laughing.